THE DOC IS IN

Erotic Stories From The Dungeon

Book 4

BJ Cuffs

While every precaution has been taken in the preparation of this book, the publisher assumes no responsibility for errors or omissions, or damages resulting from the use of the information contained herein.

Confessions

First edition. January 1, 2021

Written by BJ Cuffs.

Table of Contents

Chapter One

Esmerelda

The stark white walls were clinical, lacking any personal touches. They were in desperate need of a splash of color here or there to bring life to the landscape.

Even his paintings were nothing more than desolate tabs of color, sparsely situated on random walls, shadows hiding the small stitch of vibrant hues.

The way Dr. Brantley arranged his desk, the perfect controlled lines, everything in its place definitely signified that he was repressed sexually. The same thing could be said for many men, and women alike, when they weren't getting what they wanted at home.

My workers and I had a checklist, and it was our third day dealing with the doctor's constant complaints. Nothing was ever right in his *mistaken* opinion.

I was the recipient of the doc's tirades when he felt like lashing out at somebody.

Gail stood next to me as I worked away a smudge on the mirror in the patient bathroom, her voice barely a whisper. "I don't know what we're going to do with Sheila. I know she's the daughter of your friend, but she's not working out. I hate to be the bearer of bad news. You must have noticed that her work ethic is simply atrocious. She's always on her phone talking to her boyfriend instead of working."

My cleaning business was a revolving door of employees. Gail had been with me for almost three months. That was unheard of in our line of work. Low pay and lack of benefits made my company a temporary landing spot for many.

"There's an adjustment period we have to account for. You're probably right. I'm just not willing to give up on Sheila yet. Her mother is frantic that she's going down the wrong path. I want to give her another chance to prove herself. We all stumble and need a hand from time to time," I explained, watching Sheila over her shoulder filing her nails at the front desk.

Sheila was always malcontent, going against the grain to get under her mother's skin. The woman was crying out for help, and nobody could hear her. She was clinging to an older man that gave her that father figure she was missing in her life. It was a little weird for her to find that comfort in the arms of a mature man twice her age, but that wasn't my call.

"I don't see it getting any better. Sheila doesn't want to be here anymore than we want her to be. It's taking twice as long to get things done with her on the squad. We gave her a simple assignment, to scrub out a coffee stain in the main examining room. She didn't even touch it," Gail pointed out, her head motioning toward the room down the hall.

The one thing I hate is people not doing what they're told. This doesn't happen in the dungeon...at least not very often.

It was the first I heard of the problem, and it was just a few minutes before Dr. Brantley was going to walk through those doors to start his day.

Mondays were the worst. It only took a split second for him to zero in on a target and embellish the problem with wild gestures. His tone was not conducive to a good working relationship.

Learning his habits was one of my strengths. He was punctual to a fault. He expected the same adherence to the rules that he exercised himself every day. And he expected the women in his office to listen but not argue.

There was no denying his penchant for working his body into a temple. The fabric of his scrub pants stretched across his muscular thighs, his shirt fell against the chiseled lines of his chest, and his short sleeves were rolled so tightly I imagined he busted a seam around his biceps regularly. That physique made me want to make him my bitch. I could only wish for the day it would happen. If I didn't know better, I would have thought his gliding motions and pulse of muscles were for my viewing pleasure.

I hinted for Gail to leave as soon as possible with the rest of the squad, including Sheila. "I guess I'm going to have to take some action. That stain isn't going to clean itself. We both know how coffee stains can be quite formidable against any cleaner. It's horrible on carpets. It's a good thing I have a cleaning solution. It usually works on anything. There's not much time left. It was my idea to bring her on board. It seems only fitting that I should stick around to face the consequences."

"I don't know how I feel about leaving you to handle this. The doctor doesn't take kindly to mistakes, as we learned the first day on the job. Her probation is getting on my last nerve. She doesn't know the meaning of hard work or the value of a dollar. I blame her mother for giving her everything she wanted on a silver platter."

I didn't like people trying to conform to conventional thinking. The exception was in the workplace, where rules are there for a reason. Rules worked even in my other life. It was best to put my foot down and show them it was my way or the highway from the very beginning. I couldn't be too hard on my employees, though. I had to keep them happy when all I could afford was minimum wage.

I pushed back the pieces of hair fluttering down on my sweat peppered brow and tugged at the waist of my coveralls. The dark blue uniform I wore was simply for professional appearances.

Underneath, there was a guilty obsession hiding. Lace and satin rubbing softly against my skin.

I glanced over at Gail and sighed, nodding for the door. "We should give her until the end of the week. That way, I can say that I tried and failed miserably. Her mother will see it as a lost cause and move on to something else. I have to give her the benefit of the doubt to see if she can change her ways under my direction. I'm going to have to get personally involved."

Gail flipped her blond hair behind her ears, her long curls touching the nape of her neck. "I know you're in a tough spot. It's not easy when friends call in a favor. I've been down that road a few times to know what I'm talking about. The two of us are older than the rest of the staff. We have to set an example. Don't let her get away with murder."

I admired Gail's straightforward approach. She would make the perfect protégé to pass on my expertise in a particular field of perversion. The only stumbling block was that I didn't like mixing business with pleasure.

Those two worlds had to remain separated. Some people could be very judgmental.

They packed up without Sheila lifting a finger to help. I shook my head at how easily the new generation could become complacent. They thought they had all the answers, but they didn't even know the questions. She was what I called a work in progress.

Giving up on her wasn't an option without exhausting every measure.

The team quickly left me alone in the office with less than five minutes left before the doctor was scheduled to walk through the doors. The stain was going to get me in trouble, but it was a good excuse to sneak a look at that perfect ass the doc carried around with him.

I knelt down on the floor and pulled my bag of cleaning supplies closer. The secret weapon to the coffee stain was in my bag of tricks. It was a recipe passed down from one generation to the other in my family. A lawyer was helping me to patent the process. It was a long exhausting path to take, but I felt it was worth it in the end.

The throw rug was woven and soft, the stain sunken all the way through the fabric. It probably would have been easier to throw it out, but the Doc would have noticed immediately that it was missing. The man had a keen eye for detail. It was one of the reasons why he was the most sought after gynecologist in the area.

His lack of a bedside manner didn't prevent the women from flocking to his office. He was the best in his field. And with that title came the cockiness. He was cocky about everything from his job to the way he treated women. Why he was so popular was beyond my understanding, except for maybe the way he would look diving down between my widespread thighs.

I got down on my hands and knees in an unfamiliar position. Somebody was going to have to pay for this. I was resorting to manual labor. I was usually the supervisor, which hardly ever worked out due to my annoyingly nagging desire for perfection.

The sweetest release, though, came in the Dungeon.

The Dungeon is where I work out my issues. It's therapeutic.

All thoughts of my dark and damning abode fluttered away as I scrubbed the rug, my knuckles scraping on the fabric. The miracle cleaning solution was working, but it would take some time to lift that stain. It was time I didn't have with the ticking clock on the wall mocking me. It was painstaking work, and the effort made my arms burn.

I heard the telltale sound of a key in the lock down the hall. The very idea of the doctor standing over me in judgment gave me pause for thought.

The wreckage of his marriage was still a fresh wound. It was amazing what I could hear with my hearing aid. It wasn't as if I needed it. Nobody was aware that the handicap was a disguise to listen in on conversations. I became a fly on the wall.

A long deep sigh behind me froze my progress.

"This is the last time I'm going to say this. I hired your service for its discretion. You promised to be in and out without disturbing my normal morning routine. This is the second time I have found you in my office. I thought we had an understanding, but maybe we need to revisit the arrangement," Dr. Brantley addressed, wearing his crisp white lab coat with dark blue scrubs underneath.

"I only need another minute to get this stain out," I answered meekly, nothing like it was in the Dungeon.

"It's galling to think I'm paying good money for a service that hasn't lived up to my expectations. Is it too hard a concept for you to understand? I don't want to know you were here at all. I'm going to have to give this a lot of thought. This is very disappointing. Your assurances mean nothing to me. I don't want to hear excuses. I want to see results." He chastised me, his voice rising with each word.

It feels wrong to be subjected to his arrogant attitude. I don't like the taste of my own medicine. I wish there was some way to turn the tables. I'm just going to have to keep my eyes and ears open for a window of opportunity.

"Things like this happen and are usually unavoidable. I know what I promised. You don't have to remind me. The only thing I can do is apologize. Some things are out of my hands." I groveled to keep the contract, still on my hands and knees, looking up at him.

His hygiene was meticulous with gleaming white teeth. His dark hair was arranged perfectly without a single lockout of place, a peaking spray of salt and pepper threatening to come to life around his ears. His scrubs and jacket were pressed and clung tightly to his muscles. He believed in following the rules. Ironically, it was something we had in common in vastly different ways.

"This is unacceptable. You've already got two strikes against you. One more and I will have to look for another cleaning company. This will be the fourth one in the past six months. I thought yours would be different, but I should have known better to get my hopes up. My first patient will be here in five minutes. You better not be here when she…" He hesitated, the vein on his forehead throbbing in frustration.

His assistant Meredith was behind him, whispering into his ear about a potential problem.

He never even excused himself, walking away, dismissively, to handle the issue.

I resumed with my cleaning, scrubbing hard enough to make my fingers numb. I stopped and wiped gently back and forth and let out a sigh of relief. It was finally out without a moment to spare.

Tyrant…his wrath is fucking annoying. He thinks he's soooo important up there on his pathetic pedestal. Somebody needs to knock him back down to earth.

I used the waiting room seat to lift myself to a standing position. I was out of breath, completely exhausted. A good night's sleep with the drapes drawn during the day was my usual routine. This time, I would shake things up with a hot bath and soft music to lull my sore muscles into submission.

Glancing across the waiting room, I could see the Doc in a huff. He walked back and forth, pacing from the front door to the window without saying a word to his assistant.

I ducked back into his office before he had a chance to see me. Every time he turned, his eyes roved up and back down the perky young nurse. It felt dirty for me to stand there and witness the way that he was hungrily watching her.

I stood, my back against the wall, waiting for him to continue. It was just a matter of time before he stopped fuming internally and expressed himself with verbal commands of authority. The nurse was brave under pressure and held her head high despite treating her like a second-class citizen.

Sheila could learn a thing or two about responsibility from her. That was another problem I would have to deal with at a later date. It was essential to give her the tools to set out independently without relying on mommy's money.

I'm beginning to think the answer is right in front of me. Why didn't I see it before?

Meredith and Sheila were night and day, and each could teach the other something different.

"I don't want to hear it. This is your blunder. I pay you good money to handle these problems without bothering me. Don't make me regret hiring you. I have a simple set of standards that I require everybody to follow religiously," he argued.

"I will call and reschedule your 10:00 appointment, but the patient won't be thrilled," Meredith stated, her voice lowered to prevent any possibility of incurring his wrath.

I knew enough to know that her loyalty was without question. She was not immune to the harsh way he spoke to her, but somehow, she stood her ground. Never once did I hear her say that it was his fault. She would always find the right words without making any snap judgments.

The woman is a paragon of virtue. I just wish that he valued her in the way that she deserves.

My hearing aid was picking up something in the background. It was coming from the doctor's phone, which was left carelessly on his desk. My curiosity got the best of me, and I turned my attention to the screen. Slowly, a grin pulled over my lips.

I turned up the volume. "I see that somebody is running a fever. I have just the thing for that. Let me lift my uniform and show you where I'm going to take your temperature," the seductive female voice directed.

It appeared my strait-laced employer had a secret fetish. It revolved around being with a nurse. Now that was something I could work with.

I reached into the pocket of my scratchy blue overalls and carefully pulled out my black card with shimmering gold lettering. Nonchalantly, I pressed it to my palm and slid my hand across the slick mahogany desktop, leaving the card inconspicuously behind. It was just peeking out of the first file folder of the day.

It was going to be interesting to see what his sexual appetite revealed. His divorce was causing him nothing but problems, even if it was all self-induced from anxiety and stress. I could be the solution if he was willing to open himself to the possibilities. It stood to reason he would be hesitant, but the little voice in the head between his legs would convince him to take a chance.

I can hardly wait to get my hands on him. This won't be just for me. This will be for all the girls he has ogled and those who have felt his demeaning words. A lesson is going to be learned the hard way. I have just the outfit. It's not often I get the chance to role-play as a nurse.

I walked out of there without saying another word to him. I could almost feel his glaring eyes of disapproval boring a hole through my skull, but it made no difference to me.

He's the type of man that will have to sleep on it for a night.

The doctor has no idea what he's about to walk into, but he's not gonna know what hit him when he does. The Doctor is in, but the Nurse is gonna run this show.

Chapter Two

Dr. Brantley

The only thing better than waking up in 5,000 thread count, Egyptian cotton sheets, was waking up with a massive erection.

My eyes slowly opened up as I felt the cool, crisp sheets enveloping the mushroom head of my cock. Despite being a masturbation addict, I usually preferred a cup of coffee before my first session of the day.

With my left hand sliding underneath the sheets, I reached for my cellphone with my right one.

Should I go to my Spank Bank or search for something new?

Waking up before the alarm went off allowed me time to find some new porn, and a few clicks later, my hand was pumping away while watching a sexy nurse talk with a male patient. Her tits were definitely fake, the kind I wished the nurses at my office would get. I'd already achieved my goal of becoming the number one sought-after gynecologist in the area. If it weren't for a staff full of feminists, my other goal could quickly become a reality: sexy women in short nurse dresses, massive fake tits poking out on top, all there to service me.

It was too much of a hassle to find bimbo nurses, though.

The one in the porno slowly unzipped her tight, white dress.

"I'm afraid we're going to need a semen sample today, sir. Do you have enough in your testicles, or should we reschedule?"

The guy leaned back on the examining table as she unzipped his jeans.

"Please don't reschedule, Nurse Hannah. My balls are aching and in dire need of a release, anyway. It's just that, well…"

The nurse got down on her knees and ran her tongue along her ruby red lips.

"Let me guess: you need some help."

My fist was aggressively stroking my cock as Nurse Hannah took the man's balls in her mouth. Her long, red acrylic nails began stroking his massive cock, allowing the pre-cum to flow over her hands as she looked up at him like a chipmunk. The eagerness in her eyes was apparent as she moaned, encouraging him to produce as much semen as possible for the necessary sample.

Why can't that be Meredith???

With less than a minute until I was ready to climax, my bitch of an ex-wife sent me a text message.

"My alimony payment hasn't hit my bank account yet. Do I need to contact my lawyer, or can you man up and take care of this yourself?"

I threw my cellphone across the room, screaming obscenities as it landed upon the grey chair by the window. The same exact chair that I found my ex-wife in, where she was on her back naked and with my former business partner between her legs.

So much for her so-called low sex drive.

After transferring money into her bank account and curtly replying to her text message, I quickly got ready for work and headed into the office. On any given day, I masturbated between three to five times. Even though I wasn't above jerking off in my office, I preferred to get at least one in before seeing patients. It put me in a better mood to deal with their complaints about vaginal dryness and menopause.

My luxury sedan pulled into the parking spot labeled 'Reserved for Dr. Brantley,' and just as I was about to get out, one of my medical assistants pulled in a few places away. Meredith was relatively attractive with a full set of lips that I'd love to have wrapped around my cock, sucking, as I prepared to give her my seed. It wasn't her face or curvy body that did it for me, though.

It was her uniform.

I couldn't get away with an ultra-slutty one for obvious reasons, but the mere sight of female nurses and medical assistants gave me an instant erection.

Meredith slipped out of her car and headed inside, bending over when she accidentally dropped her keys onto the pavement.

Fuck, I want to pound that ass!

The only other vehicles in the parking lot were from the cleaning crew, all of whom were inside, so I said 'fuck it' and began jerking off. My balls filled back up with cum in no time as Meredith swiped her key fob along the outside of the door, bending over one more time and giving me a perfect view of her cleavage.

I beat my meat so fucking hard while picturing my cum coating those tits, rope after rope saturating her skin as she begged for more.

"Fuck! Fuck! Fuck!"

My black leather steering wheel turned bright white within a matter of minutes. Gobs of my seed slithered off of it as I caught my breath, realizing that was the first time I'd ever masturbated outside.

My blood pressure lowered slightly as I made my way inside, but not enough to prevent me from becoming livid at the cleaning crew. There was the owner, on her hands and knees scrubbing out a coffee stain in the middle of the waiting area. I had told her multiple times that I did not, under any circumstances, even want to see them working.

Every woman should be on their fucking knees in front of me, though.

I cleared my throat loudly as she continued scrubbing, although I did enjoy seeing her body tense up at my presence. The woman knew she had fucked up yet again.

"This is the last time I'm going to say this. I hired your service for its discretion. You promised to be in and out without disturbing my normal morning routine. This is the second time I have found you in my office. I thought we had an understanding, but maybe we need to revisit the arrangement."

"I only need another minute to get this stain out," the woman answered meekly.

"It's galling to think I'm paying good money for a service that hasn't lived up to my expectations. Is it too hard a concept for you to understand? I don't want to know you were here at all. I'm going to have to give this a lot of thought. This is very disappointing. Your assurances mean nothing to me. I don't want to hear excuses. I want to see results."

"Things like this happen and are usually unavoidable. I know what I promised. You don't have to remind me. The only thing I can do is apologize. Some things are out of my hands."

I straightened my white jacket while looking down at her.

"This is unacceptable. You've already got two strikes against you. One more and I will have to look for another cleaning company. This will be the fourth one in the past six months. I thought yours would be different, but I should have known better than to get my hopes up. My first patient will be here in five minutes. You better not be here when she…"

Meredith's perfume hit me before she leaned into my ear.

"We have a problem, Dr. Brantley."

I followed Meredith out of the waiting room until we were alone, eyeing her up and down. It was hard to concentrate on what she was saying, though. All I could think about was how I'd just climaxed all on my steering wheel while thoughts of her on her knees raced through my head. The only thing I got was some problem with the schedule for that day.

"I don't want to hear it. This is your blunder. I pay you good money to handle these problems without bothering me. Don't make me regret hiring you. I have a simple set of standards that I require everybody to follow religiously."

Meredith lowered her voice and mumbled something inaudible.

Since I had some time before my first patient, I pulled the porn back up on my cellphone and went into my office. Nurse Hannah was still sucking the guy's balls and stroking his cock, something I desperately wanted Meredith to do to me. Just as I was about to jerk off again, however, I was needed at the front desk.

Once again, I angrily tossed my cellphone, pissed off that another masturbation session was being ruined by some needy woman. To add fuel to my raging fire, the only reason I was needed was that the bimbo secretary had locked herself out of our computer system.

If only I could get her in a nurse's uniform.

I arrived back at my personal office a short while later, happy that the cleaning crew had finally left but pissed that I no longer had time to jerk off. However, upon pulling out my first patient's chart, a black card with gold lettering fell onto the ground.

Mistress Esmerelda - The Dungeons

Which one of our office temps is moonlighting at an adult bookstore or club?

I might have been a masturbation addict, but at least I didn't visit seedy establishments.

Forty-five-year-old female, experiencing menopausal symptoms, vaginal dryness…same shit, different woman.

The black and gold card was making me curious, though. I hadn't been to an adult bookstore, let alone any club in ages, and as a medical doctor, I couldn't risk being seen in one. For shits and giggles, I searched the business online, but nothing came up. A reverse address search simply stated that it was a local business with absolutely nothing to do with sex.

Now I really need to know what the fuck this place is.

After hitting a few buttons to hide my cellphone number, I called the one listed on the card.

"Thank you for calling The Dungeons. Are you looking to set up an appointment with a Dominatrix?"

Chapter Three

Esmerelda

The next 24 hours made me anxious. I couldn't sit still when I was home alone, thinking about what I would do to Dr. Brantley. Visions of the naughty things I'd do to him flowed through my mind as I tried sleeping that night, envisioning him in all sorts of positions. Dr. Brantley would beg for mercy as I brought him to his knees, making him feel submissive for a change.

That next morning, I didn't see him at the office and was out of there in plenty of time, despite Sheila lagging behind. We were making up for her shortcomings and lack of direction. She thought she was going to skate through, but she was in for a rude awakening. Somebody fierce and not willing to bend was going to make a world of difference.

It was something I had discussed with her mother at length over the phone. She was admittedly hesitant but understood the importance of learning about the real world. It was fortuitous for there to be an opening in the doc's office.

Meredith found a scathing letter about Sheila that I had handwritten for her and left on the desk when I went for the day. It pinpointed those places Sheila could work on and how Meredith could be of service. I detailed my admiration for Meredith and how she could be instrumental in giving the girl the gift of her experience. Sheila was going to have to dig deep to let her true self free. Besides, I was sure a familiar friend in the medical industry would do me right somewhere along the way. And Meredith could move some of the doc's wrath over to Sheila, lessening her load a bit.

But that was the last thing on my mind by the time I made it to the Dungeons that night. I had plans, and I was already setting them in motion. I stood lips pursed, staring around the space, imagining all the different toys I would eventually add to my collection.

Celeste popped her head into my room.

"A little birdie told me you're going to have a unique visitor.

Please don't break him, though. Women depend on him for a clean bill of health, if you know what I mean. Apparently, he walked in on his former business partner going down on his now ex-wife. Or so the rumor mill has it. He does come off as an arrogant prick, so don't hold back too much…" Celeste trailed off, temporarily distracted by my latest acquisition.

I smirked and stepped to the side, giving her a better view of a real medical examiner's bed with the traditional stirrups.

"I saw this at an auction and couldn't pass up putting a bid on it."

"I'll bite my tongue, but remember that anonymity is something that we take very seriously around here. Then again, your clients always come back for more."

"Tonight is about using kid gloves while still giving him what he wants, and you should know by now that I pride myself on being professional. I'd rather my own identity be exposed rather than any of my client's."

She smiled and whistled a familiar tune while heading out the front door.

As a pioneer in professional domination, Celeste was smart in purchasing part of the business. She didn't know, and I wasn't about to tell her that I had a 10% stake in the company, not including the compensation I received from my clients.

The echo of light knocks on the door filtered through the still room.

Before opening the door, I put on my black Venetian face mask and applied one more application of red lipstick. Dr. Brantley surprised me by wearing an immaculate Italian suit. The white shirt added a touch of sophistication, and the cufflinks completed the look. His cologne was overpowering at first but soon became an aphrodisiac for my olfactory senses.

"Good evening, Dr. Brantley. Please, come in and make yourself comfortable."

I pointed to the chair in the middle of the room, which was bolted to the floor. Dr. Brantley eyed me up and down in my black leather dress that fell to my mid-thighs, fishnet stockings, and classic black stilettos.

Dr. Brantley sat down nervously, fidgeting with his hands in his lap.

"I'm not really sure why I'm here, Mistress Esmerelda."

I let the door shut slowly, worried that any sudden movements would send him bolting.

"This place is a cone of silence. There's confidentiality here that I don't take lightly, Dr. Brantley. Just look at my mask."

I stood behind him as I moved my leather-clad hands through his hair, slowly and lightly pulling at the locks.

His involuntary moan captured my attention.

"This isn't something that I'm proud of, but I masturbate about five times every day, Mistress Esmerelda."

I walked back around to his front, placed my hand on his knee, and pulled a chair close to him.

"I'm sure there's more to it than chronic masturbation, Dr. Brantley. That's the clinical term…to make you feel more comfortable. There's no reason to hold back, though. We can address your issues by finding constructive solutions."

"It's been driving me crazy lately. What human being doesn't have a secret fetish they don't want to talk about with their significant other in this life? It's amazing what women will talk about when I have them in the stirrups. My business requires discretion and adherence to the Hippocratic Oath to do no harm," he confessed, his body relaxing and his mind slowly opening to the possibilities.

I leaned forward and began massaging his muscles, fully aware that he was staring down my cleavage.

"Keep going, Dr. Brantley."

He closed his eyes.

"I…I…I've always been fascinated with nurses, Mistress Esmerelda. To explore those thoughts would require revealing something about me that would make things awkward. It started out as wanting them to submit to me, but sometimes…"

I whispered seductively into his ear, my fingernails digging a little bit deeper into his shoulder muscles.

"Sometimes what, Dr. Brantley?"

"Sometimes I fantasize about them controlling me, Mistress Esmerelda."

"I want you to do me a favor and keep your eyes closed. It doesn't matter what you hear; they must remain shut the entire time. I promise you it won't hurt a bit. You can trust me with your deepest and darkest desires. Stay right there and don't move a muscle."

"I should leave," Dr. Brantley said suddenly, trying to get up despite my hands keeping him in the chair.

I leaned forward and whispered to him, our lips just inches apart.

"You could do that, but you would regret it for the rest of your life. We all wear blinders to what we really want in life. You have this one chance to make your fantasy a reality. Don't let your courage to admit your weakness be for nothing."

I went into the changing room and quickly found what I was looking for. It was already in plain sight, waiting for me. The white latex with the red stripe accompaniment, including the nurse's cap, was a nice realism touch. It was very snug and rubbed against my body, sending electrical charges of excitement through my thighs.

The surgical mask in baby blue would hide my identity. It was my time to bring out the Mistress.

I stepped back into the room to find Dr. Brantley sitting in the chair with his eyes closed. Walking around him, I leaned forward and parted my lips, letting my warm breath trickle down his neck. Goosebumps rose as I rounded toward his ear, gently blowing against them. He shifted and squirmed, breathing heavily.

The man was under my spell, and we were just beginning our journey together.

***

The Doc

As I stood in front of Mistress Esmerelda's door, it occurred to me that perhaps an Italian business suit hadn't been a good choice. The Dungeon was where men went to live out deviant sexual fantasies, not listen to a priest speak. In my defense, however, I had never been to a BDSM club before.

I gently knocked on the door after counting to ten, which did little to calm my nerves.

What if one of my patients sees me here???

Mistress Esmerelda opened the door, revealing herself to me in a black half-Venetian face mask and lips redder than Meredith's.

"Good evening, Dr. Brantley. Please, come in and make yourself comfortable."

She pointed to the chair in the middle of the room, which was bolted to the floor. It was hard to see straight with her in that black leather dress, fishnet stockings, and classic black stilettos.

I sat down nervously, fidgeting with my hands in my lap.

"I'm not really sure why I'm here, Mistress Esmerelda."

"This place is a cone of silence. There's confidentiality here that I don't take lightly, Dr. Brantley. Just look at my mask."

Mistress Esmerelda didn't give me much time to look at her, though. Within seconds she was behind me, running her leather-clad hands through my hair slowly and pulling at my locks.

Why the hell am I so fucking nervous???

"This isn't something that I'm proud of, but I masturbate about five times every day, Mistress Esmerelda."

She walked back around and stood in front of me again, placing her hand on my knee and pulling a chair closer to him. All I wanted to do was have her extract my semen like Nurse Hannah had done in the porno.

Mistress Esmerelda leaned so far into me that I had no choice but to look down the front of her dress, practically drooling at her luscious cleavage that would look even better covered in my cum.

"I'm sure there's more to it than chronic masturbation, Dr. Brantley. That's the clinical term…to make you feel more comfortable. There's no reason to hold back, though. We can address your issues by finding constructive solutions."

I licked my lips, daring her to kiss me. She didn't take the bait, though.

"It's been driving me crazy lately. What human being doesn't have a secret fetish they don't want to talk about with their significant other in this life? It's amazing what women will talk about when I have them in the stirrups. My business requires discretion and adherence to the Hippocratic Oath to do no harm."

Oh, but I thought about breaking that Hippocratic oath on several occasions.

Mistress Esmerelda leaned forward and began massaging my shoulders, giving me an even better view of her cleavage.

"Keep going, Dr. Brantley."

I closed my eyes.

"I…I…I've always been fascinated with nurses, Mistress Esmerelda. To explore those thoughts would require revealing something about me that would make things awkward. It started out as wanting them to submit to me, but sometimes…"

She whispered seductively into my ear, her fingernails digging a little bit deeper into my shoulder muscles.

"Sometimes what, Dr. Brantley?"

"Sometimes I fantasize about them controlling me, Mistress Esmerelda."

It was the first time I'd ever admitted to wanting to lose control.

"I want you to do me a favor and keep your eyes closed. It doesn't matter what you hear; they must remain shut the entire time. I promise you it won't hurt a bit. You can trust me with your deepest and darkest desires. Stay right there and don't move a muscle."

It suddenly occurred to me that my former business associate, the gynecologist who was having an affair with my wife, could be around the corner. The rumor mill had been rampant in town, and everyone in the medical community knew what she'd done to me.

"I should leave!"

Mistress Esmerelda kept her hands firmly on my shoulders, though.

She leaned forward and whispered to me, our lips just inches apart.

"You could do that, but you would regret it for the rest of your life. We all wear blinders to what we really want in life. You have this one chance to make your fantasy a reality. Don't let your courage to admit your weakness be for nothing."

The sound of her stilettos upon the floor filled the room, and I grappled with what I should do. If I hadn't been aroused, I'd have booked it out of there and never looked back. Hell, I'd even burn the fucking card that was left in my office.

I never did figure out who left it there, either. Nor did I recognize the sultry, sexy voice of Mistress Esmerelda. No woman I knew sounded anywhere near as hot as she did.

My pride kept me seated, though. Mistress Esmerelda was right. I would be stupid to let my courage for admitting my weakness be for nothing, and if that bastard wanted to out me to the medical community, then so be it. Who would believe him, anyway?

Everyone in our field looked down on him, anyway.

Goosebumps popped up all over my skin as the sound of Mistress Esmerelda's heels filled the room again. Her warm breath trickled down my neck as I shifted and squirmed in my seat, breathing heavily.

This woman has me under her spell, and I can tell that we're just getting started.

***

Esmerelda

It felt like an eternity waiting for Dr. Brantley to open his eyes. The sexual tension between us became stronger with every passing second, with both of us wondering what would soon transpire.

"I bet you know what I'm wearing, Dr. Brantley, and it's better than you could ever imagine. A little realism mixed with the fantasy is what's going to make this an experience you're never going to forget," I said in a throaty, deep whisper of seduction.

The hairs on the back of his neck stood on end. He softly bit his lip, dragging his teeth across the surface. Dr. Brantley kept his eyes closed, though, and remained silent.

"The one thing I need to remind you is that you have free will. The door is always there for you to use if you feel this is going too far. There's also the safe word which we should come to terms with. Pick something unique to you," I urged, the white latex glove brushing his lips until he was sucking on the tip.

"Code red…" Dr. Brantley blurted out, his eyes blinking me into focus.

My nipples stood at attention as he scanned over my body.

"I have something to show you, but first you must get undressed. It's not like I haven't seen a cock before, mind you, so there's no reason to be embarrassed. Just do what I tell you, and everything will go smoothly," I insisted, my hands on the small of Mr. Brantley's back.

He slowly disrobed until he was in his underwear, stalling out of fear. I grabbed his black silk boxers, pulling them down to his ankles in one smooth motion. Dr. Brantley's cock sprung to attention, bouncing and slapping against his stomach.

I snapped my fingers and pointed toward the examination table.

"I need to check your cock and balls extensively. A good physical requires a thorough approach, which I'm sure you can appreciate."

Dr. Brantley nervously climbed onto the examination table. I examined his cock and balls, happy to find them without hair or any kind of blemish. Taking a firm hold of his shaft, I stroked the length, applying pressure at the base with my other hand.

I worked his pliable flesh with both hands as his head fell back, and he was overcome with pleasure. Dr. Brantley jerked and twisted to the rhythm of my fingers, moaning as his balls became larger by the second. When his grunts went up an octave, I slapped the shackles into place before he had a chance to react.

His eyes flew open in shock as his muscles bulged and rippled, jerking defiantly against the chains.

"Wait… What's going on?"

"What's going on is you're now under my care, asshole," I stated, one hand still manipulating his little head into submission, the other trailing my nails up his chest.

Chapter Four

The Doc

The longer Mistress Esmerelda stood in front of me, the more I wanted to open my eyes. She already knew my kink: nurses. Sexy, smokin' hot nurses who are in complete control of my orgasm. So what were we waiting for?

She took a step closer until, knowing damn well that she was teasing me.

"I bet you know what I'm wearing, Dr. Brantley, and it's better than you could ever imagine. A little realism mixed with the fantasy is what's going to make this an experience you're never going to forget," I said in a throaty, deep whisper of seduction.

The hairs on the back of his neck stood on end as I pictured her in a nurse's uniform, hopefully, one that showed her gorgeous curves. My cock was beginning to ache as I imagined her inspecting my manhood just like Nurse Hannah had done in the movie. The Alpha male in me started to come out, though.

I was getting in over my head.

The longer I sat there, waiting for her to reveal herself, the more aroused I became. And the hornier I got, the less control I had.

I softly bit my lip, dragging my teeth across the surface to stop myself from speaking up. If I said anything, it would be 'adios' as I hightailed it out of there. After having come so far, how could I abandon my fantasy?

My eyes remained silent as Mistress Esmerelda continued.

"The one thing I need to remind you is that you have free will. The door is always there for you to use if you feel this is going too far. There's also the safe word which we should come to terms with. Pick something unique to you."

I was still on the brink of getting the hell out of there, but then she brushed my lips with her white latex glove, and I knew there was no escape. Mostly when it slid into my mouth.

"Code red…" I blurted out, my eyes blinking her into focus.

Holy fucking shit, she's hot in that uniform!

Her nipples stood at attention as I scanned over her body.

"I have something to show you, but first you must get undressed. It's not like I haven't seen a cock before, mind you, so there's no reason to be embarrassed. Just do what I tell you, and everything will go smoothly."

Her hands rested on the small of my back.

I slowly disrobed until I was in my underwear, stalling out of fear.

This is crazy. I'm definitely packing a massive cock! Why am I still so nervous?

Mistress Esmerelda grabbed my black silk boxers, pulling them down to my ankles in one smooth motion. My cock sprung to attention, bouncing and slapping against my stomach as pre-cum splattered everywhere.

She snapped her fingers and pointed toward the examination table.

"I need to check your cock and balls extensively. A good physical requires a thorough approach, which I'm sure you can appreciate."

I nervously climbed onto the examination table.

This is it, man. There's no turning back.

Mistress Esmerelda examined my cock and balls, seemingly happy with what she saw. She took a firm hold of his shaft, stroking the length and applying pressure at the base with her other hand. I had received dozens of hand jobs over the years, and Lord knows I wasn't new to jerking off, but feeling those latex gloves grip my dick was better than all of my sexual experiences combined.

Mistress Esmerelda worked my pliable flesh with both hands as my head fell back, too overcome with pleasure to even think straight. My body jerked and twisted to the rhythm of her fingers, moaning as I felt my balls getting larger by the second. However, when my grunts went up an octave, cold, steel shackles wrapped around my ankles and wrists.

What the fuck have I gotten myself into???

Esmerelda

It was amusing to see him frantically pulling at those shackles and chains with nobody around to judge him. Dr. Brantley looked up at me in a blind panic, practically begging for some kind of explanation.

I pointed out the heat of his arousal at its full potential, bulging at the veins.

"There's no reason to get all bent out of shape over nothing, Dr. Brantley. This is how you learn to find pleasure from your pain. Plus, I'm wearing exactly what you requested."

His head shook back and forth, yet his erection remained the same size.

"I'm not sure about this, Mistress Esmerelda. We never discussed shackling me to the table! It's dawning on me that you had this planned from the moment I stepped into the room," Dr. Brantley said, looking around at the other implements hanging from the wall, including whips and riding crops in varying degrees of sizes and shapes.

I addressed his naked prone form with my eyes laser-focused on his manhood.

"I wasn't lying when I told you that you could leave at any time, Dr. Brantley. The door is right there in front of you. Say the safe word, and we'll never see each other again. Is that what you really want, though?"

Pre-cum continued leaking down the sides of his shaft, creating a very delicious-albeit obscene-ice cream cone.

His delicious cock aside, Dr. Brantley didn't appreciate what I'd called him.

"Fair enough, but why did you call me an asshole? You don't know me well enough to make that kind of assumption.

I lifted the white latex of my nurse's uniform very slowly.

"I've known men like you all of my life, Dr. Brantley. You're all the same."

It wasn't until I revealed the soaking wet evidence of my arousal that his cock twitched in response. I climbed on top of him, allowing my panties to rub against his throbbing manhood. I was filled with an overwhelming desire to consume him.

Dr. Brantley tried shifting several times by angling his body, hoping to catch the fabric with the head of his cock. I allowed him a brief fantasy of slipping it into me. It lasted no more than a minute before I gradually slid my wet crotch over his abdomen and then lightly grazed his nipples, making him squirm.

Using a pair of surgical scissors from a nearby table, I ripped my panties' wet crotch lining in half.

"I want you to worship my asshole, Dr. Brantley. You will get a treat for doing a good job."

Dr. Brantley began licking his lips feverishly, finally accepting that his fantasy was becoming a reality. All he had to do was allow himself to submit, and he'd officially become my sex slave.

"I don't know why, but I want you to smother me with your beautiful round globes," Dr. Brantley pleaded.

It encouraged me to settle in for the long haul.

I rubbed my ass cheeks against his face until he pressed his nose into the cleft, feeling his hot breath against the rosebud of my asshole. Dr. Brantley's cock began thrusting up and down, begging for some form of release, as he worked his tongue deep inside of my glorious asshole.

"Don't you dare touch my pussy, Dr. Brantley! The only excitement that I'm going to derive from this experience is through anal. There's more to a woman than her pussy wrapped around your cock, you know. We require a lighter touch with a little bit of finesse."

He grunted and groaned, sending that vocal vibration throughout my body. Despite enjoying every second of it, I wanted more out of him.

"I'm going to need you to do better than that. Use your hands to really get in there. There's enough slack in the chains for you to hold onto my cheeks!" I directed while at the same time I pinched Dr. Brantley's nipples and pulling them away from his body.

Treating his tongue as an exciting new sex toy, began bouncing up and down on, encouraging him to go even further. I was careful not to drown him, though. It didn't serve a purpose to let the orgasm overtake me in a moment of weakness. Keeping it simmering on the surface was an excellent way to acquire his reckless attention to detail.

Both hands were latched onto my cheeks, his fingers pressing into the pliable flesh. Dr. Brantley was an eager little fuck.

A moan escaped my lips while fighting back an orgasm.

"I could easily get into a position where we are both pleasing each other at the same time, but why bother? Doing so would only distract you from your current task."

Dr. Brantley mumbled something incoherent, his face too smothered by my ass cheeks to get a word in. As much as I wanted to make the moment last, my body was in desperate need of satisfaction. I hated that I would give him what he wanted, but I had needs too.

I once again began rubbing those lips now exposed against his shaft. Hovering there in a stalemate had me in the driver's seat. I was committed to making him a prisoner of my advances with promises of retaliation if he didn't follow my directions to the letter.

There was something in the way that he rolled his eyes when I dropped my weight. There was no way to stand up on my own 2 feet after experiencing the battering ram of his insistence. It spread me open with my hands on his chest.

I suddenly grabbed his hair and made him look at me through those tiny slits in his eyes.

"I want to make one thing perfectly clear, Dr. Brantley. This isn't for you. You can't blow your load without my permission. I can get off as many times as I want. I might show pity, but only if you show me the kind of stamina that I'm looking for in a slave," I said, my body slowly rising and falling while creating a vacuum around the base.

"I will do my best, Mistress Esmerelda," he whispered.

"I do have to admit that I like this can-do attitude. Just don't disappoint me. The last thing you want is to find out what my bad bedside manner looks like. You are running out of time. This session is rapidly coming to a close," I moaned, a motion of my head toward the clock on the wall signifying there were less than 10 minutes left before I was going to give him the boot.

I was putting my heart and soul into everything I did to break him of his bad habits. He had to learn to control those basic urges. Lowering the dress to show him my breasts was playing dirty. Those nipples were ready to be consumed into his mouth.

I cradled his head and felt the slippery surface of his tongue circling my left nipple.

This is too good to be true. Dr. Brantley is better than I thought. I have to wonder if he knows how to please a woman. There's a reason why he's alone. Color me curious to learn more about what makes this man tick.

I was picking up the speed with long drawn out strokes to make me feel every inch of his impressive endowment. It had to be nine inches. It filled every part of me and pressed against the walls, slippery to the touch.

Working him back and forth with my movements becoming labored was becoming tedious. As I felt my climax reaching its full potential, it came over me with a tidal wave of warmth spreading throughout my body. The scream emanating from my mouth was muted by three inches of solid steel and three feet of a brick wall.

I took that prolonged pleasure on the balls of my feet. Dr. Brantley's immense physique was turned on beyond a shadow of a doubt. He was soon doing his part by thrusting his pelvis to get that maximum penetration.

This is the perfect time to question him about his lovemaking skills.

"I'm guessing you are here out of necessity. Tell me the truth. Do you satisfy a woman?" I asked, already knowing most men would lie through their teeth to save face.

I stopped moving when I felt that vein throbbing.

"It pains me to admit that it's one of the main reasons why I can't seem to keep a woman in my life, Mistress Esmerelda."

I began riding him hard and fast while slapping his chest to spur him on. I came again, this time with my fingernails scratching his chest deep enough to leave a mark.

He was almost there when I took away the object of his desire: my pussy.

The sharpened knife of his pain and pleasure came in the form of my hands repeatedly slapping his cock head.

"I'm going to let you go, Dr. Brantley. You'll have the freedom to jerk off for me. Don't do it until I give you the signal, though," I urged while still standing there with my hand between my legs.

Dr. Brantley quickly took that one hand and went to work on his column of flesh. It breezed up and down the length, using the wetness of my hole to pave the way. He had a good rhythm, but he had to stop several times to keep time with me. His entire body began convulsing as he shot his load all over his stomach, making a rich portrait in his hot cream.

I found it a necessary reserve of strength to jump on top of him at the moment of my sweet relief. The squirting evidence of my hungry need sprayed everywhere. It was covering him from his lips down to his mighty depleted member.

Dr. Brantley walked away with the promise to return at his earliest convenience. I waited until he walked out before collapsing to my knees with my hands on the cold concrete floor.

Chapter Five

The Doc

My leather office chair pressed firmly against my back, but instead of appreciating its comfort, all I could think about was how Mistress Esmerelda's breasts had felt back there. Soft yet firm, seducing me with both her sensual femininity and eagerness to be my Alpha. Against my better judgment, I had confessed my perverted fantasies and masturbation addiction.

With arousal came vulnerability.

She knew what she was doing.

Images of Mistress Esmerelda had since taken up permanent residence in my brain. With my face buried between women's legs in stirrups, I kept wishing that it was *me* on that exam table instead. 'This patient will be different,' I told myself before going into each room. 'It's only because the ones so far today haven't been that pretty.'

Bullshit.

The majority of my clients were Trophy Wives whose husbands were also in the medical field. How many times had I wanted to plunge my cock inside of them as they told me about their gynecological issues?

Of course, you're experiencing vaginal dryness, honey. What else did you expect when you married an old fart just for his money?

I, on the other hand, was in the prime of my life and could easily fuck these women into orgasms that would transform their legs into wobbly noodles, stumbling out the door as they left my office. It's precisely what Mistress Esmerelda had done to me at The Dungeons.

Meredith poked her head into my office, watching me stare at the computer screen for a few seconds before speaking.

"Dr. Brantley, do you have a few moments?"

"Yeah, sure. Whatever."

The sight of her in scrubs usually aroused me, even when I was in a shitty mood, but not anymore. All I saw was my medical assistant, who just happened to be female.

"Your next and final patient of the day had to reschedule, but before you get mad at me, please listen to her reason."

I shrugged my shoulders apathetically.

"That's fine. We'll just close early. Let the front desk know."

Meredith's eyebrows went up as she nodded and left me alone again with my thoughts.

I went home that night intending to masturbate myself to sleep, but it was useless. Every time I got hard, Mistress Esmerelda's voice crept back into my brain, and I couldn't focus on getting off. I needed her magic touch, and it was driving me fucking crazy. When watching Nurse Hannah jerk a male patient off into a semen cup didn't do the trick, I searched for different videos with other women. I came close with a busty brunette milking a man's prostate but stopped just short of an orgasm.

Without Mistress Esmerelda, my masturbation sessions had become pointless.

Fuck!

Out of sheer desperation, I closed the porn and called The Dungeons.

"Thank you for calling-"

"I need to see Mistress Esmerelda tonight."

"I'm sorry, sir, but she's not available tonight. Mistress Esmerelda does have an opening-"

"No, you don't understand. I need to see Mistress Esmerelda right away!"

"Sir, please calm down. She has an opening tomorrow evening at seven o'clock."

Since when did I have to adjust my schedule for a fucking woman? It should be the other way around!

"Sir, are you still there?"

My balls had reached the aching stage.

"Look, I don't think you know who I am, but not seeing her tonight is *not* an option."

I could sense the woman smiling through the phone.

"You're not the first man to say that, sir. Do you want the appointment tomorrow evening or not?"

It was the closest to crying that I'd ever come.

"Fine. Goodnight."

"Wait, I need your name, sir!"

In a rush to get my attention, the woman's voice had slightly lost its sensual touch and sounded oddly familiar.

"I'm a doctor."

"Look, we pride ourselves on anonymity. *Which* doctor are you?"

"When I arrive tomorrow night at seven o'clock, just tell her the doc is in. That's all she needs to know."

***

Esmerelda

My surprise didn't come from the Doc wanting to do it again so soon, but from making him follow the rules from the pleasure. It was unparalleled compared to my other clients. Dr. Brantley was one cocky, arrogant asshole who was long overdue for a wake-up call.

Celeste stood in the doorway of my room at The Dungeons, eager to talk about Dr. Brantley.

"I saw him this morning."

"What do you mean you *saw* him, Celeste?"

"He's my gynecologist. Anyway, he's usually all business and doesn't talk much about his personal life. This time, however, he got to talking about his divorce. I actually found myself empathizing with him."

I wasn't quite sure why, but knowing that Dr. Brantley was her gynecologist didn't sit well with me.

"Well, it's not like he knows what we look like behind these masks. Just make sure you don't let your dungeon-voice slip into your real one. You know what I'm talking about."

Celeste placed her finger and thumb on her lips before zipping it closed.

"Believe me, you have nothing to worry about. I don't need a man I'm paying to poke around in my vagina knowing I work here. However, you should know the other girls like to gossip."

"How so?"

"Let's just say they like to take a sneak peek when they hear a door opening in the Dungeon. I'm sure you are guilty of the same thing," Celeste eluded with her hand, motioning to the other doors down the hallway near my own.

I nervously chuckled while zipping my lips closed, just as she had done. Celeste and I weren't close friends. On the contrary, it was merely our insatiable desire to dominate men and the occasional women that united us.

"I refuse to incriminate myself."

She did a double-take of my white latex nurse's uniform.

"I'm not going to ask any questions, but I think I get the idea.

It's a little predictable for Dr. Brantley to want that certain fetish.

Just keep him on a short leash and don't succumb to temptation at the wrong time. These men need to learn their place."

Celeste disappeared into one of the vacant rooms down the hallway dedicated to her brand of domination. I took a few minutes to read over instructions I found online about using ASMR during a jerk-off session, which stands for an autonomous sensory meridian response. Basically, a person is overcome by a tingling sensation by listening to certain sounds. In my session with Dr. Brantley, it would be the sound of my voice.

He walked in without knocking a few minutes later, which was his first mistake. The frustration on his face told me that he was in no mood to play games, almost like he was ready to punch something.

Dr. Brantley lowered his voice to an almost inaudible decibel.

"I'm terrified that I'm becoming addicted to you. It's affecting the way that I treat my staff."

I lifted his chin to see his anger slowly subsiding.

"I want you to take a few deep breaths, Dr. Brantley. This is not the time to bring the outside world into this environment. In here, everything is forgotten except for my words echoing in your ears. This is a milestone in your life, and you should be taking it seriously. A man is nothing without a firm hand behind him, guiding his pleasure and pain. I want to begin by having taking off your clothes."

He was about to say something but thought better of it, realizing that I really didn't want to hear about his problems. Those things were better left to therapists. His mind wasn't what I was interested in when his body was crying out for direction.

I whispered into a microphone, my eyes focusing on his as speakers amplified my voice throughout the room.

"This is something I borrowed from one of the other girls in the Dungeon."

Dr. Brantley's face lit up, although his words were starting to slur a bit.

Looks like someone's been hitting the bottle to deal with his divorce.

"I like where this is going. It's not easy to forget about how people constantly disappoint me. One woman, in particular, gets underneath my skin. I'm guessing from your expression that you don't want to hear me speak unless spoken to."

I watched him strip to the skin.

"She sounds like a real bitch, but let's leave her behind for the evening."

He sat down on the same chair with his hands at his sides.

He looks vulnerable for the first time in his life, waiting for me to start the proceedings. The awkward silence of the clock ticking on the wall is turning me on. His patience is wearing thin, but I don't care.

I maintained the same low, throaty whisper while speaking into the microphone.

"I want you to begin by getting to know your cock. Use your fingers to trail over the flesh but don't apply too much pressure. Let the teasing gesture of that stolen contact take you by the throat. Spread your legs and use this tingling lubrication. We don't want any friction burns."

As much as I enjoyed using the microphone, my body yearned to be closer to his.

"Close your eyes, Dr. Brantley."

"Yes, Mistress Esmerelda."

I quietly walked towards him, my heels clicking upon the floor to mimic the sounds I'd heard in several ASMR videos. Standing behind him, I slowly wrapped a blindfold over his eyes and whispered into his ears.

The result was instant goosebumps all over his arms and thighs.

"There's no reason for you to see me when you can rely on your other senses, Dr. Brantley. Take your cock in your hand and stroke it slowly. Don't be in a rush to finish this time. We're going to build up your tolerance over and over again. I will warn you that it is going to be painful and exhilarating in a way that you can never imagine."

He wrapped his fingers around the base, unable to touch. It was relatively thick and demanding.

I walked in front of him, making him release his shaft long enough for me to place the cock ring. It was a teaching tool to keep him raging strong with all the blood trapped inside. He didn't question my authority and went back to stroking in the same slow movement I had ordered him to do.

"I've never done anything like this before, Mistress Esmerelda. Can you please go back to whispering in my ears?"

I stood behind him as he requested, whispering into his left ear this time.

"That is my hand, and that is my cock to do with as I wish."

"Yes, Mistress Esmerelda. This is your hand, and this is your cock to do with as you wish."

I could smell the heat of the exchange in the air. It was rather pungent and quite titillating. Dr. Brantley got the hang of what I was trying to do without much direction.

"That cock is an extension of my body, and I have complete control over it."

"Yes, Mistress Esmerelda. This cock is an extension of your body, and you have complete control over it."

I continued whispering, going back and forth between each ear.

"I want you to speed up for ten strokes and then stop abruptly. That's it…really put that hand to work. The expression on your face is fucking hot."

Dr. Brantley did precisely as I'd instructed.

"Use both hands with one going over the head on every stroke. Do this for a full minute at a medium pace. Use more of that tingling lubrication if necessary. We don't want you to dry out. It's more pleasurable when it's slick."

My lips were practically touching his ears whenever I spoke.

I couldn't help but feel empowered to lift my dress with my finger poking underneath the crotch of the panties. That time they were crimson in pure leather. Plunging knuckle deep had me moaning into Dr. Brantley's ears while he was stroking to my amusement.

"I know it hurts, but you are doing remarkably well for the first time. We're going to have to revisit this very soon. Don't stop. This time do five fast strokes and three slow ones. I know that you are feeling lucky to be in my presence. That's the way that it should be. I do enjoy seeing you squirm and drip hotly all over your hand."

Dr. Brantley's body language was practically screaming for release, twitching and convulsing with every stroke of his hand and word from my mouth.

"I'm going to count you down from 10, Doctor Brantley. When I get to zero, you better be ready, or you leave here with no release. You might want to touch yourself after the fact, but you are forbidden to do so without me there to witness it. It might seem cruel and unusual, but you have to learn to follow the rules. You've always been a stickler about rules. It must seem strange to have the tables turned in my favor."

He was frantically moving his fingers in a blur, barely recognizable with the naked eye as I slowly counted down. It was going to be a quick delivery. When I reached zero, his knob expanded before pulsating with a geyser of foam into the air. The first shot went directly into his gaping mouth. He was shocked but stayed with his mouth open, taking another shot before the intensity diminished.

He immediately spat it out onto the floor. Dr. Brantley was both disgusted and secretly fascinated by what had just happened. I just hoped it wasn't the beginning of the end.

I watched him run until he was clutching his clothes on the way to the door.

"Who owns your orgasm, now?" I said in a much louder voice, eager to put him back in his place.

There was a moment of reluctance until he finally relented.

"You do, Mistress Esmeralda."

The force of his climax was one of the biggest I had seen in quite some time. It rivaled some of the times I had pegged guys. It did give me a reason to explore new territory with him, though.

***

The Doc

I nearly fell over my feet while getting changed in the hallway. That orgasm had been, without a doubt, the most intense one I'd ever experienced. Mistress Esmerelda's nurse's uniform would have been enough to make me blow a hot, sticky load all over the floor, but then she had to add in that ASMR stuff.

What is she doing to me?

I had every intention of high-tailing it out of there, afraid of what another minute would do if I remained seated in that bolted-down chair. Mistress Esmerelda knew that I was a masturbation addict. She knew that I had no problems jerking off upwards of five times per day. Hell, I could probably knock out eight if she pushed the right buttons.

And that scared the shit out of me.

Yet even the subtle change in her voice as she called after me, which also sounded vaguely familiar, sealed the deal that she absolutely owned my cock and balls. Without her instructions, I would never allow myself to jerk off again. I wanted her to completely control me.

I stumbled to the reception area, contemplating whether I had the balls to schedule another session.

Oh, get over yourself. You're in too deep now, doc.

"I'd like to schedule another session for tomorrow night."

The woman behind the desk tilted her head at me.

"So soon, doc? Are you sure you can handle it so many times in a row?"

"Yes, same time tomorrow, please."

I didn't even wait to see if there was another man scheduled. If I showed up and she was with someone else, then I'd pay both her and them handsomely. Mistress Esmerelda might own my orgasm, but as a man, I still had needs.

I made myself a sandwich and played my voicemails once I got home that evening. The only one that stood out to me was from my lawyer regarding the divorce.

"Hey, it's me. Look, we really need to talk about the alimony payments. Your ex-wife has decided that she deserves more and said something to the effect that her father loaned you money to start your business. We're talking about a substantial increase, by the way, so call me back right away. Even if it's after midnight."

That bitch can take my entire paycheck because all I care about right now is Mistress Esmerelda.

Chapter Six

Esmerelda

Dr. Brantley was a few minutes late that evening, which was hypocritical for a man with a pet peeve about punctuality. It didn't bode well with that he might be having second thoughts about our sessions together, either.

He came in and sat down in the chair without a word exchanged between us. It took some intuitive thinking to know what he was struggling with. Missy was the best at reading those subtle clues. She taught me a few tricks, including being aware of my surroundings at all times. Especially during my emotional climaxes where I couldn't see straight for a few minutes.

I have to wait for him to come out of his shell. This has to come from him. His imagination must be running wild, with many different scenes playing over and over again in his head.

"I almost canceled this appointment, Mistress Esmerelda. What happened last night was a first for me. I'm not talking about the denied gratification, either. I'm just not sure how to say the words."

"Just say it, Dr. Brantley."

With one deep breath that made him fall back against the chair, he confessed what I'd already suspected.

"I want to eat my own cum."

"I'm sure that was a hard admission for you, Dr. Brantley. Although, that seems remarkable since you have access to the equipment 24/7/365."

"Wait, have you had other guys say they want to eat their own cum?"

My head fell back as I laughed.

"Are you kidding me? Every guy has at least thought about it. Now, tell me what's stopped you from doing it."

Dr. Brantley cleared his throat a few times before speaking again.

"I've always wanted to, but I've chickened out too many times to count. It happened by accident last night. I swear that I wasn't trying to aim for my mouth. Is there any way you can help me?"

I moved a life-like dildo back and forth between my hands, wondering how he'd react to the rubber phallus.

"There might be a way for both of us to get what we want. This is an old friend of mine, and he's been asking about you. I know it's an inanimate object, but it really does feel alive in my hands. His name is Elvis."

Dr. Brantley shook his head back and forth as I walked over to him, lightly pinching his nipples through his starched black shirt. His little yelp from the slight pain was comical.

"I'm not sure I'm ready to get fucked by a dildo, Mistress Esmerelda, let alone one named *Elvis*."

"Silly doctor, you should know by now that you don't have a choice. Well, you do on some level. All you have to say is your safe phrase, Code Red, and all of this is over."

Dr. Brantley licked his lips, realizing that he was too far invested to pull out now.

I stood back and pointed to his body.

"I knew you'd stay. You've already forgotten the golden rule when you come into my room, though: the clothes don't remain on. This is the last time I tell you without punishment."

Once he was naked, I took his hand and showed him to the makeshift stockade until his hands and head were firmly entrenched within it. He was lying on his back on the wooden table.

It won't be the last. I get a kick out of fueling the desires of my slaves. It's almost enough to give me an orgasm without touching myself. I'm not quite there, but being with him is slowly loosening my restraints. Stepping up behind him greets me with those half-moons.

I opened him up with my fingers while applying a liberal amount of water-based lubricant down the shaft, then did the same to his ass crack, letting it find its way using the path of least resistance.

I was hit with an immediate jolt of excitement when I slapped both of his cheeks at the same time. He jumped but remained silent, with only a slight whimper in response. He was learning to keep his mouth shut. It was good that I didn't have to use more extreme measures, but it was also a little disappointing.

"It might not sound plausible, but I'm going to fuck the cream out of you. There's a reason why your legs are free. I think you can guess what I'm going to do," I mocked, my hand underneath Dr. Brantley's knees until his legs were attached to these chains hanging from the ceiling.

His rampant condition was hovering over his open mouth. It almost touched but not quite. That particular concept was going to need a little bit of patience and training. To get over that hump would mean stretching him out further than he had ever been in his life.

"I almost forgot one important detail," I said with a snap of my fingers.

I left him in that position, awkwardly bent like a pretzel. Retrieving the item and fitting it into his mouth to keep it as wide as possible made him look at me in fear. That was what I was feeding on when I started to press the issue with Elvis's big head.

It took a concentrated effort, but it finally started to slip past the ring of resistance. It was a very tight squeeze. Breaking his cherry and forcing him to face his biggest fear was exhilarating. His hands and head were immobile, giving me plenty of opportunities to take him on a journey of self-discovery.

Every inch wasn't wasted on him. His cock was extremely hard and was flexing every time that I gave him another inch. The continuous flow of warm cream was pooling across his tongue in long sticky strings. It was a prelude for what was to come.

With my body in the right position, I got to work on pegging Dr. Brantley with Elvis.

"I'm gentle by giving you time to adjust, Dr. Brantley. Elvis is anxious, but I'll reel him in. The king has not left the building just yet. I can move my hips, but I don't do what he can do onstage justice. This is my way of keeping his memory alive in a different way. There…you have all of it, and you didn't think it was possible."

That recognizable pop was followed by me forcing it back in. Dr. Brantley must've been feeling the exertion on his calf muscles, but the man wasn't complaining. It wouldn't have done him any good if he had tried, anyway. It wasn't like he could talk with that metal contraption stretching his jaws wide.

My hips began moving a little bit faster while hitting that one spot he probably didn't even know existed, despite being a doctor.

"I know it's not very comfortable, but you did want this. You never said how I could go about it, either. You might say I have taken a creative license. The asshole is fucking tight, especially yours! I only wish that I could feel what others of your gender takes for granted. This is a dismal comparison, but I can still revel in the power of taking you like this."

His body remained grounded on the table, his legs high in the air. The feeling was indescribable to have him at my mercy. Adding more lubricant was necessary, though. It was long-lasting but still dried up over time. Keeping it slick and slippery was my gift to him.

The justice of punishing him for his bad behavior toward women wasn't lost on me. It served him right for falling into my trap, too. Typecasting him as an arrogant prick had proved to be the correct assumption.

Dr. Brantley was grunting every time that I bottomed out, with not one inch being spared from the dark recesses of his asshole. His grunts turned into low whimpers and finally into unrestrained passionate moans.

My aphrodisiac was seeing the length of Elvis going in and out of him, watching his asshole clamp down around the invading force inside of him.

"I have to tell you that I've had other men in a similar position screaming for mercy. This is just a drop in the bucket. I have other things that I want to do that I haven't even mentioned. It would help if you were very careful about who you trust. You never know how some people might take advantage of your naïveté."

It was nice to be in a quiet space where he couldn't say much of anything with his mouth wide open like that. Every time I hit that spot, his cock would jerk in response. He was listening to a universal language of pure unadulterated lust. It was not a dream, and he would have to get used to the reality of being under my control.

His breathing was getting faster, with his chest heaving in response to what I was doing to him. Those sensitive nerves inside were being ignited. Keeping things fresh by moving at different angles would show him how important it was to mix things up. Continually changing the rhythm and momentum was keeping him on edge. He was unable to find the moment that he would scream at the top of his lungs.

"I think you know by now that it's never easy with me. I'm going to give you what you have come for, but it will be on *my* timetable. That might not seem fair, but it's not like you can do anything about it. You can't even say the safe word with that thing in your mouth. Your eyes convey fear and excitement," I said with a sharp jab.

I was unable to let him go when I was feeding on the adrenaline of his fear. I figured there would be time for apologies after the fact. Sometimes it was better to ask for forgiveness than permission. It was even better when he jumped at the opportunity to be used by me.

I was sweating with the effort and decided that it was time for him to face the music. Turning the switch and initiating that first vibration had him squirming and groaning with defiance.

I quickly attached a cock ring to the base of his member.

The cock ring kept him from losing it prematurely until I was ready to take things to the next level.

I lowered my voice into the ASMR one I'd used on him the night before.

"I have tightened it around the base to make it impossible for you to find relief. Your balls are bloated. It must be painful. Please, tell me that it's painful with a slight nod of your head to confirm my suspicions."

He was able to move his head a couple of inches. That was the green light I was looking for to really put the screws to him. Stopping and catching my breath gave me a moment to see the excitement in his eyes change to fear all over again.

His ass had closed up, but it wouldn't take much to reopen him for business.

I now have complete control over his orgasm.

He suddenly burst and almost choked on the volume that was shooting into his mouth. In that position, he couldn't spit it back out and was forced to swallow it for the first time in his life.

I came without any form of stimulation other than watching him take it deep and relentlessly. I couldn't even get up to escort him to the door after releasing him from a trap of his own making.

I can hardly wait for the next time.

Chapter Seven

The Doc

The receptionist had been right the other night. Seeing Mistress Esmerelda so many times in a row had been a bit too much. I hated not being able to focus on anything other than her gorgeous face and body, with those luscious curves in that nurse's uniform. That's why I canceled our appointment the following night.

My ego had also been severely bruised when she got me to climax while fucking me up the ass with Elvis.

Elvis. Who names their fucking sex toys?

The woman of your dreams, that's who.

And then she made me eat my own cum. In her defense, I hadn't bowed out of being in that position. I knew damn well it was coming, the taste of that sweet but salty creamy concoction. Finally, I knew what women had tasted all of these years.

Mistress Esmerelda made my fantasy come true, and that scared the living shit out of me.

I chugged another beer, silently wishing it was my cum instead while reading over documents from my lawyer. My ex-wife's father had, in fact, loaned me money to start my medical practice. She wasn't wrong, and that ate me up inside. The alimony payments to her would be going up substantially just to pay it back.

If only I could have just given it directly to her father instead of her, though. I was a man of my word and had every intention of paying him back, but it shouldn't go through the person who ripped my heart out. Out of all of the women I'd ever been with, she was the only one I had fallen in love with.

Until Mistress Esmerelda came into my life.

I shimmied out of my clothes and took a long, hot shower, hoping it would clear my mind. It didn't, though. By the time I climbed into bed, I was riddled with guilt for bowing out of our session. But I refused to fall into another woman's trap. I refused to become addicted to another woman's touch, especially after confessing to so many sins.

My cellphone began ringing right as I was about to watch another Nurse Hannah porn, and this time it was my ex-wife.

"What the hell do you want, Danielle?"

"I want to know if you signed the documents, *Daniel*."

I hated that our names were so similar.

"All communication is supposed to go through our lawyers, so technically, you could be in a hell of a lot of trouble right now. Maybe I'll use this to get out of giving you more money!"

Danielle let out a low, throaty chuckle into the phone, which actually made my balls shrivel up.

"And maybe I'll expose you for all of your perverse fantasies, Daniel. I can't imagine that would go over well with your colleagues."

"You mean the one you were fucking behind my back?"

"Just sign the documents, Daniel, because I'm looking for a new car. Goodnight."

I threw my cellphone across the room, surprised when it didn't shatter into a million pieces upon hitting the wall.

Danielle had walked in on me jerking off in the bathroom one night, back when we were married, to a Cum Eating Instructions porno. We never talked about it, but I found several hidden cameras throughout the house after filing for divorce.

I could only imagine the dirt she had on me. Needless to say that when it came to alimony, she had me by the balls. And now that I was becoming obsessed with Mistress Esmerelda, it occurred to me that I didn't want two women pulling on each of my nuts at the same time.

I rolled over to go to sleep, eager to start fresh the following day at work. I had a busy schedule, with back to back appointments of Trophy Wives complaining about their vaginal problems. Eventually, I would forget all about Mistress Esmerelda and what happened between us at the Dungeons and go back to my somewhat normal life.

I just hope the fucking cleaning crew isn't there when I show up tomorrow morning.

Chapter Eight

Esmerelda

I wasn't surprised when Dr. Brantley didn't show up for his next appointment. He mistakenly thought that he had gotten everything out of our sessions, but we had barely begun the slow journey of his degradation.

I was the woman with power in the palm of her hands, and he was my work of art of a sex toy.

It was almost laughable for him to think that he could walk away without my permission. It was the first time I had considered revealing my identity to anybody outside of the Dungeon, too, which was a milestone that I didn't take lightly.

Sheila was no longer employed by me and was now under Meredith's watchful eye; they were a match made in heaven. Meredith didn't take any nonsense and ran a tight ship, plus there were no personal phone calls allowed in the office. It put a strain on Sheila's relationship with her boyfriend, but I took up the slack in that department.

She didn't need to know how her boyfriend was seeing me on the side. He was no longer going to be a controlling prick dictating the terms of their relationship. They would be on a level playing field, and she had *me* to thank for it.

The cleaning staff was there when I arrived to supervise, but I really wasn't needed. My team soon left with a hefty bonus. Nobody questioned why I stayed behind in his office either, sitting in his chair with my legs up.

I had made a conscious decision to contact his assistant by text message that morning. She was under the impression that he was the one asking her to come in later than usual. It probably came as a shock, but she wasn't going to question the message's validity.

It was a wonderful feeling to be sitting there in my maid's uniform, waiting for him to step through the door. He would have a few choice words, of course, and I would be ready with a snappy comeback along with a shocking revelation.

Dr. Brantley would feel like hell after I was done with him. It was the way that it should be. The man was not strong enough to resist me, and I would take advantage of that. I was everything he wanted and more, but he was not in a position to sever our connection.

There was no reason to lie to him when the truth would serve my purpose.

The door to the office opened, and then I heard his footsteps approaching. Those Italian loafers had soft soles, but I could still listen to them shuffling down the hallway.

Dr. Brantley opened the door and let out an angry gasp as I spun around in his chair.

"What the hell are you doing in my office, woman? How many fucking times do I have to tell you that you will be gone by the time I arrive? Are you looking to be fired or something?

I let out a low, throaty chuckle in the same voice I used at The Dungeons.

"It's not nice to walk out on me, Dr. Brantley. That is something that I can't stand for. You are a smart man. That much cannot be denied. Surprisingly, you haven't put the pieces together. Doesn't my voice sound familiar to you? It should, considering we have spent time outside of this office together. Perhaps, a visual aid will help you to understand better."

I stood up and slowly began unbuttoning my uniform, showing small pieces of the nurse's outfit underneath.

He stood there planted in one spot, watching me with a confused look until he finally blinked with recognition. There was no disguising his startled deer in the headlights look.

I took a few steps closer to him.

"I'm sure you think this is some vivid dream, but I can assure you…it's real. Did you really think you could walk away from me without facing the consequences? The woman who has cleaned your office and introduced you to Elvis is one and the same. That cock between your legs doesn't belong to you anymore, Dr. Brantley.

Now make your mistress happy and take it out. Let it hang outside of your fly, and don't you dare touch it."

He licked his lips nervously as his cock began to harden from within his pants.

"My assistant will be here any second! I'm begging you, Mistress Esmerelda, to please stop this insanity!"

"Don't you think I've taken care of Meredith? I made an arrangement for her to come in at noon with Sheila. We have a couple of hours and will take full advantage of it. Now, drop your pants and your underwear at your ankles."

He swallowed hard and did what he was told without making a stink about it.

It's the influence of my hand that makes him jump. I've trained him well. It makes me proud to know that he is my property. I didn't bring Elvis, but I got the next best thing without it being too conspicuous in my purse.

The vision of what I was going to do to him was forming into a delicious scenario. Manifesting my destiny by taking the Dungeon and bringing it to him was a stroke of genius. There was nothing complicated about a locked door and two consenting adults doing what came naturally.

"I had high hopes for you, but you disappointed me. It was expected. The last few days have taken their toll on you. I hate to see you reverting to old habits.'

I attached a leash and brought him into an examination room across the hall.

With his cock standing straight up, Dr. Brantley got on his knees and bowed his head.

"You don't understand, Mistress Esmerelda. I desperately need to keep my two lives separate."

"Pfft, I know that it's more than that, Dr. Brantley."

He took a few moments to find the words.

"Fine. Look, Mistress Esmerelda, I'm getting too close to you! The last time that happened, I got hurt. Really bad. I mean, you don't know what that evil woman put me through! Now that bitch has me by the balls, and so do you!"

I crouched down so that I was a few inches away from his ears.

"You forget one important difference between your ex-wife and me, though, Dr. Brantley. You *want* me to have you by the balls."

I slowly reached down and began cupping his nut sack, causing pre-cum to spurt out like hot lava.

"Oh God, Mistress Esmerelda. I ambit your humble servant at your mercy!"

I pulled a dildo out of my purse and held it in front of his face.

"This should teach you it's better to work *with* me than against me."

I want him to know what is going to happen without saying the words. He's going to come to his own conclusions by the way I'm slapping that appendage in my hands.

He protested with his eyes wide at the implication of walking by this room every day and remembering what I did to him.

"You can't be suggesting…not here…not now."

I laid down on his examination table to get comfortable while holding onto the base of the dildo, waiting for him to comply.

"I want you to have a constant reminder. I'm just trying to figure out what position I want you in. I think this time you should sit on my cock. That way, you can walk by this room and remember how you bounced on top of me."

He looked around nervously before slowly surrendering his body to mine. Dr. Brantley climbed up with his knees on either side of me, then applied some of my tingling lubrication to the dildo. After poking and prodding for a few minutes, his eyes bulged out as I hit the target.

I used my hips to make him realize it was my game to play.

"You're not leaving this room until you take every single inch! It's not as thick as Elvis, but it's certainly longer. It will be able to delve deeper into the dark recesses of your soul. Your shame is nothing compared to my pleasure from seeing you on top of me like this. Go ahead and make me proud by being the little bitch I know you can be!"

The upbeat tempo when he moaned his submission was putting me in a good mood.

"You can jerk off for me while I sit on your face and fuck you with this thing," I muttered, my breath coming in long gasps.

That was only the beginning.

I was soon sitting on his face getting the full extent of his long tongue and fucking him at the same time with the dildo. It wasn't long before I was squirting all over his face with my juices dripping down his chin and filling his mouth. It remained wide open for my pleasure.

He didn't have to jerk off when I could do it for him with my other hand that remained free. It happened quickly, and I continued to pump his meat until he was shooting it everywhere. His deep groan was captured inside of me to prolong my pleasure until I finally gave him his body back.

"I have the leverage of you doing some interesting things on video. You are going to show up tomorrow night on time. I think you know what will happen if you don't. Bring your ATM card. You are going to need it to make it up to me," I said while pulling down the latex material and walking out of his office.

It's a risk to reveal my identity, but the orgasm I just had makes it worth it.

Chapter Nine

Esmerelda

I decided to try something different, capitalizing on Dr. Brantley's guilt for standing me up. It was going to depend on his willingness, though. The whole idea came to me in a dream. It made sense and would show him that he wasn't above punishment.

My fascination with big cocks wasn't exactly a secret. I wanted something that I couldn't have. I made some inquiries with my fellow mistresses in the Dungeon. They were rather amused and gave me one name unanimously. Their praise for his endowment and the legend of his stamina excited me, and soon Dr. Brantley would be there to witness my fantasy come to life.

Twelve inches was an estimated size.

I was standing in front of him, completely fixated on the bulge between his legs. It wasn't even hard yet and hung there limply, looking more formidable than most men at their full potential.

I have never wanted anything more. Dr. Brantley is a divine gift. I'm not going to waste this chance. He'll just have to shut up and watch.

Wearing a tight pair of jeans and no shirt, Carl confessed his concerns about what was about to happen.

"I know what you want, and I have to admit this is foreign territory for me. I'm not sure how I feel about fucking you in front of somebody that can't touch you. You are damn gorgeous in that red leather, though. I've always been a sucker for women in leather boots."

He tried touching me, but I feigned interest by giggling under my breath. Being a little breathless in the presence of a man was uncommon for me in my chosen profession.

Feeling a strong desire to worship at the altar of his magnificent beast, I took a few steps back.

"I don't have to take this fresh stuff. Just keep it in your pants until Dr. Brantley gets here. It won't be long now."

Carl's eyes lowered to an expanding problem stretching out the fabric of his denim jeans.

"I'm taking my cue from you, ma'am. You can't blame a guy for wanting to be with you, though."

I directed him to the closet.

"Stay out of sight until I require your presence."

He nodded and went inside just as Dr. Brantley showed up, walking in and getting undressed without any coaxing.

"I need to apologize, Mistress Esmerelda. I feel horrible for standing you up. I'm ready to pay for my transgression in whatever way you deem appropriate."

I pressed my hand against his chest.

"I've already billed you, but that's only part of it. I think you need to know your place. Another man is going to come in here to fuck me. You are pathetic, and I need a *real* man with a *real* cock to satisfy my urges. That's why you're going to become a cuckold."

Dr. Brantley tried standing up, but my hand kept him seated. I saw the look in his eyes. He wanted it. Hell, he was practically begging for it. But that stupid ego of his was getting in the way.

His cock stood tall at attention.

"That's not what I signed up for! My ex-wife did the same thing, and it ruined our marriage. She could never look at me the same way after seeing me grovel on my knees while watching her satisfy another man, and then I came home one night to find her getting fucked by my business partner!"

I motioned for Carl to come out of hiding.

"What I'm hearing is that she made you feel small. What I'm *not* hearing is anything that would indicate you didn't like it. Your mistress knows what you are trying to hide from her. It's not what you say but what you leave out. You most likely claimed to feel ashamed, but deep down, you loved every minute of it."

Dr. Brantley was above average, but he still failed in comparison to Carl's cock.

I grabbed Carl and began stroking the log between his legs. It was something that made me a slave to my desires. I fell to my knees while pulling down the zipper of the red leather bodysuit, exposing my breasts.

He slapped that big piece of meat between them, and I folded the flesh around his trembling equipment. It was easy to recognize a man with an obsession for big breasts. He was already showing signs of his arousal with droplets of persuasion in sticky nectar clinging to my skin.

I whispered into the head of Carl's cock and stuck my tongue out, eager to taste that warm cream.

"I want you to look at this man, Dr. Brantley. You will *never* measure up. I think the plain truth is hard to deny. The one thing I don't need is a man that can't last long enough to satisfy me. This is the answer to the problem. I don't care if you like it, but I know you do. That thing between your legs might satisfy most women, but I'm not like most women. I need something more than the average man. This is unreal."

I grabbed it at the base and turned it slightly toward Dr. Brantley, half expecting a complete surrender to his fundamental nature. He shook his head, and I wasn't going to press the issue. It was good enough that he was here stroking in front of me while I was about to go down on Carl.

Carl stopped me by grabbing my hair. It was the first time in a long time somebody else had taken control.

"I don't want your mouth. Just stand up and bend over in front of Dr. Brantley! I want him to see the look on your face when you feel my cock burying itself deep within your folds. There's a concern you won't be able to take the full length of it. I've had similar worries in the past. I've come to understand women can stretch to accommodate just about anything within reason."

Carl lifted me to my feet until I was bent over, touching my knees and looking at Dr. Brantley.

I moaned with my eyelids fluttering in response to just the head pressing into me. Some women couldn't care less about the size. The visual component of seeing him in his prime was making me wet.

He steered that piece of granite into my body. It felt like something was tearing me apart from the inside out, but not in a bad way. An idea came to me while I was taking it from behind, his hands on my hips.

I'm not sure how he's going to feel about it, but he will do it despite any inside objections. This beast is showing me a good time, but it can be better.

"I want you to crawl underneath me and lick my clit, Dr. Brantley! It's not nice to keep me waiting, either."

He took a deep breath and found himself on his knees, pressing his mouth to my mound. The first tentative touch of his tongue made me quiver. The walls closed in around him, rhythmically squeezing his large and intimidating hardware.

It wasn't easy to stay in that position. I was getting firsthand knowledge of what I put my subjects through.

"How do you like having a real cock to satisfy those cravings? You really don't have to say anything. The sounds you're making are more than enough," Carl stated with thrust after thrust followed by a lengthy pause still buried inside of me.

His breathing was in long deep gasps.

I would have chastised him about his lack of stamina, but I was already a hair-trigger. When he began again less than a minute later, his energy was without question a runaway train with no brakes. The hard slap of his hips reverberated back to me. Every time he bottomed out, my body reserved the right to have a mini climax.

Dr. Brantley was feverishly stroking his cock in front of me, straining the muscle in one arm to stay in the perfect position to eat me. I dropped, and he collapsed underneath me until I was sitting on his face.

His body jerked, and the excitement level had reached a breaking point. He fired off into the air, just barely missing my face after almost twenty minutes. The fountain of his cream continued in varying degrees of intensity for nearly a full minute.

Seeing him getting in touch with his voyeuristic need pushed me over the top.

I want him to see it from his vantage point from between my legs. That orgasmic rush forces me to accept the reality that big pieces of lumber are my weakness.

Dr. Brantley continued to draw out my pleasure with his mouth latched to my clit.

The steel pipe inside me was bulging obscenely. I could feel every inch expanding, especially the head. That pipe burst as he grunted into my ear while unloading the volume from his balls.

I can feel every spurt, and I want more. I demand more, and I'm going to get it.

I pointed to the camera, which had recorded everything.

"I'm not saying you're never going to touch me again, Dr. Brantley, but the odds are against you. Come back tomorrow, and you can watch me with him again. I might take pity on you, but I wouldn't count on it. We don't need you anymore this evening. I want you to go home and think about this new cuckold relationship. We both know you will be back or suffer the consequences."

Dr. Brantley nodded and quickly got dressed.

"I will be back, Mistress Esmerelda."

The door closed behind him, and I turned my attention to Carl. His depleted member was rising from the ashes of his orgasm.

"I was going to say that I wasn't finished with you, but it appears you echo that sentiment," I said with a smile.

I fucking love my life.

Epilogue

Esmerelda
1 year Later

It had been another long evening at the Dungeons, where I had five back to back appointments with new slaves. Each one was different, though, which kept me on my toes. There was the guy with a foot fetish; the one who wore women's underwear at his construction job; the one who wanted to be in permanent chastity; the one who was eager to try pegging; and the one who tried to follow through with eating his own cum.

The last one, for obvious reasons, was my favorite.

I pulled into my driveway, eager to have dinner with the love of my life. The past year was the complete opposite of how I thought my life would turn out. Never in a million years did I ever expect to be in a long-term relationship, mainly because of what I did for a living. And especially not with the man I ended up with.

But there he was, standing at the stove cooking one of my favorite meals.

"I absolutely love coming home to you, Dr. Brantley."

He squeezed my ass cheeks while passionately kissing me.

"You know, I do have a first name."

"I know, Daniel. I just prefer to call you doctor."

We sat down to lasagna with homemade noodles and sauce, Italian salad; breadsticks; and a bottle of fine wine. Dessert wouldn't be food that evening.

"Are you excited to celebrate our first anniversary tonight?"

Daniel nodded while enjoying the fruits of his labor in the kitchen.

"I'm incredibly excited. It's a new venture for both of us and right up my alley. By the way, you know you don't have to work so many late nights anymore. I bought the place from you as a gift because you deserve to relax more."

"I know, darling, but it keeps me on my toes. Plus, I stay busy as you work your late-nights at the hospital. Talk about a major career move."

We spent the rest of dinner talking about our future plans and how lucky we were to have found each other. It was hard to believe that I was Daniel's cleaning woman a little over a year ago, whom he chastised for being in the office whenever he arrived. And there he was, ready with dinner on the table after I came home from a long night at work.

After dinner, the two of us went upstairs and got ready for the second part of our anniversary.

Daniel took my hand and brought it to his lips.

"Are you ready, darling?"

"Absolutely."

***

A short while later, I opened the door to my room at The Dungeons and was pleasantly surprised. There was my slave for the evening. Restrained in cuffs and a ball gag in his mouth, he waited patiently for me on his knees.

"Oh, my. I have quite the treat for you tonight, my little pet."

My slave grumbled, unable to speak due to the ball gag.

A few minutes later, Daniel walked in shirtless and a pair of leather chaps, black latex gloves, a black leather mask, and holding a pair of nipple clamps. My slave's eyes bugged out with excitement.

"You're going to be in good hands tonight, my slave, and do you know why?"

He shook his head back and forth, eager for me to continue.

"Because the doc is in."

Wild Erotica From BJ Cuffs

Reader,

Thank you for taking the time to read The Doc Is In: Erotic Stories From The Dungeon Book 4 Make sure to grab your copies of the other three books. And don't go just yet, the next few pages are a sneak peek at the The Dungeon Part II....The Stacks. Sexy Librarians are exactly what we need.

You never know where the whip will land next.

The Stacks: An Erotic BDSM Story
<u>Chapter One</u>
Goodie Two Shoes

Okay, missed that one… one more time then.

The library catalog wasn't going to organize itself, though I often wondered how, with all the technology we had, it didn't automate. Then again, by the stale brown indoor/outdoor carpet and wood chairs from the '70s, it shouldn't be such a shocker that I was still standing there cataloging. The bell on the library's front door chimed, and I looked up to see Mrs. Mathews entering.

She was short, white-haired, and had been coming in for book selections long before I ever started working there. She was really sweet, though, and I was told her husband died five years before. Reading was what she did to pass the time. My heart ached for her, but at the same time, I couldn't imagine a marriage like that in the current world. I had done my fair share of dating, and by my mid 20's, I found myself utterly exhausted. Between the high maintenance and the million different ways a man, or woman for that matter, could cheat, I just gave up.

"Hi Missy, how is everything?" She greeted, in her usual chirping tone.

"It's good, how are you? Are you done with my last recommendation already?"

"I'm a fast reader," she chuckled. "Thank you for the recommendation though, I absolutely loved the book."

"I'm glad you liked it," I said with a smile, feeling a sense of pride only a librarian could understand.

"I have always liked noir characters. You know, when you can't really decide whether to root for them or hate them– there's just a gray area where you're satisfied and sad by whatever the ending brings you."

"Well, Mrs. Mathews, recommending books can be nerve-racking, so I make sure the person really gets what they want."

The library I worked at was one of the biggest and most visited in the city. Getting a job there was exciting but exhausting. My love for books and old architectural libraries made it worthwhile, though.

"You're sweet. It's good to see old fashioned, plain nice people. They are basically going extinct, aren't they?" Mrs. Mathews chuckled as she searched through her purse for her library card. "I mean, imagine you were as mean as all those other people. You know, the tough know-it-all types who basically tell other people what to do."

"Yeah, that would be very hard to imagine," I said with a smirk, which went unnoticed.

I turned toward the counter, pulling down on the hem of my thin mint green sweater over top of my white collared full sleeve dress shirt. With a plaid skirt and dark mint green heels, my look was 100% what my best friend liked to call "librarian chic."

My blonde hair was down and rested in soft waves at my shoulders, and my bright hazel eyes were accented with just a touch of makeup.

"Well, alright, sweetie. I won't take much of your time. I know you're busy." Mrs. Mathews sighed as she handed me her card.

I scanned it and the new book and handed them over with a smile. "I'll see you next week, Mrs. Mathews. Be safe."

"You too," she replied poignantly.

"Excuse me." A voice sounded behind me as soon as Mrs. Mathews walked away.

I turned around to find a girl, probably in her mid-teens, blushing as she brought her hands together.

"Hey, how can I help you?" I responded warmly, smiling at her.

She reminded me of myself back when I used to be such a timid and shy girl. Now?... Well, that's a whole other story.

"C-Could you guide me to the f-fiction area, please? I've been looking for it and can't find it."

How cute. A young me.

"Sure, come on, I'll show you."

Another day at my job at the library. And I loved it. I showed the girl the fiction section and recommended a few of my faves from when I was her age. Then, though it was the one part of my job I hated, I headed back up to finish the cataloging for the day.

"Hey, Missy! Where have you been?!" Jennifer, my best friend, popped up next to me, with zero control over her vocal levels as usual.

"I am like a foot away from you right now. You really don't have to yell," I complained, flinching a little.

People turned to look at us, but one glare from Jen, and they resumed their reading. The woman surely would get us kicked out of there one day. But it was her vitality and excited personality that kept me on my toes, and I loved her for it.

"Yeah, so what? I'm your best friend, and a girl's allowed to be excited to see her best friend." As always, she turned more adamant rather than accepting her fault.

"Why do I even bother." I rolled my eyes with a playful jab in her ribs. "And might I remind you, we work in the same building. How could your excitement build-up to that octave in that small amount of time? I would definitely be deaf if you met someone famous or found your long lost dog from childhood."

"Hey," Lola, one of the other librarians whispered, poking her head between us. "You mind covering the desk for a second? My mom's on the phone. I don't know, something about summer vacation plans and my father's insistence on decorating the basement with road signs. She's having a mom meltdown."

I chuckled and nodded. "Of course. You can't plan those kinds of emergencies."

Lola rolled her eyes and shook her head as she walked from the building to take the call. Jenn and I took the seats behind the desk, leaning back for a moment off of our feet. We never got to man the desk, and especially not together. I glanced over at Jennifer. "Aren't you supposed to be in your section?"

Jennifer rocked back and forth in the office chair and gave me a shrug. "Meh, it's boring over there. Anyway, so, back to my expressive vocal abilities. I may be loud, but I think I have the right to demand to know where you were."

"I was right here with you all day, at work." I tried to divert even though I knew what she was really referring to.

I had been avoiding the conversation ever since meeting up with her that morning for coffee. However, thankfully, we had a busy day, so neither of us had time to catch up… until then. I was still trying to figure out a story to tell her. I had to get better at that. If I was going to have a secret hidden life even from my best friend, I needed to have excuses ready to go when she asked.

"No, not this morning," she replied, giving me an accusatory look. "The night I called you like eighteen times but got your voicemail every single time. I was about to call the cops thinking someone had abducted my poor, sweet, innocent librarian, but then I figured they'd most likely bring you back. You know, when you started talking about 17th century English literature."

"Come on, girl. You've known me for quite some time now. I go to sleep early and then come back here in the morning. That's basically my life. And the stories behind the authors in the 17th century can be riveting and provocative, I'll have you know." Attempting to divert Jennifer's knowing glare, I nodded at Lola as she returned to her post with a smile of gratitude on her face.

"Thanks girls, crisis averted."

I headed back to my station and Jenn followed, not even skipping a beat.

"Yeah, how could I forget. You're basically the poster child for sexy librarian…only…minus the sex." Jennifer laughed, following me as I pushed a cart full of books toward the different stacks along the back.

"Okay, maybe my life isn't as eventful as yours, but at least I don't laugh at my own jokes."

"Well, that's because I'm so funny. In reality, with your dating record, or lack thereof, I really should be weeping for you." Jennifer gave me a pouty look. "And speaking of hot sexy dates…"

"We weren't actually speaking of hot sexy dates," I replied.

Jennifer ignored me and continued talking. "I was calling you because Dave was coming over last night, and since your makeup and outfits are always on point, I wanted some help."

I stopped dramatically, fanning myself. "Is this my lucky day or what? My best friend pays me an actual compliment, and I get asked to do makeup so she can go get laid. Sounds like a wonderful…long blow right to the junk."

Jennifer giggled, and several people shushed us. We held our laughter, disappearing into the stacks. Jenn sighed and looked at my outfit. "I mean you have a gift with clothes. Although, I'm still baffled trying to figure out what exactly you do in these clothes. Your life is the library, and then, even when you begrudgingly go home, all you do is drink coffee and read."

I turned and put my hands on Jenn's shoulders. "You know, if you start helping me shelve these books while you try to unlock the mysteries of my existence, we'll get done quicker." "You know," Jennifer continued, ignoring my exhaustive sigh as she tapped her chin. "With the kind of fire you have at times, you should definitely do something besides wasting away in the dusty stacks of the library. I mean, the only eligible men here are either old, or I can picture them spending their days at a tech company, and their nights wearing someone's skin suit."

I had to stop myself from laughing out loud. If she only knew what my life was really like. She'd definitely lose it and then want to join the club. Instead of laughing, I settled for an amused smile instead. But telling her my secrets wasn't on my radar. She was too loud with secrets, not to mention that it was almost more fun when I kept it all to myself.

My dirty little secret.

Suddenly, one of the more timid of librarians, Steve, stuck his head around the corner. His hair was disheveled as usual, his white button-up only half tucked in, and his corduroy pants looking like he had purchased them two decades before. "Hey Missy, I need you for something."

It was the kind of day where everyone needed me for one thing or the other.

"Yeah, everything okay?"

"Well, yes. For now. But your services are needed," he said with a nervous twitch. "Jimmy is here."

"Oh, Jesus. Not him again," I exclaimed, pinching the bridge of my nose.

"Look, I know it's bad, but you seem to be the only one he responds to. I tried and failed miserably. And now we depend on you." Steve gave a nervous grin as I sighed, walking past him. "Think of it this way, you'll always have job security."

"Sure, if I don't kill Jimmy first," I grumbled under my breath.

"Can't we just ban him or something? He could go to other libraries and be a headache for them." Jenn suggested, jogging excitedly next to me.

"We can't. Believe me, I've tried. Besides, how many people read these days anyway? Yes, he's always late turning in his books. Yes, he talks down to the staff. And yes, he complains about every self-inflicted fee he acquires, but sometimes, I think he does it on purpose."

Jenn snorted as we approached the desk. "He probably gets off getting you all super librarian and everything."

I cringed at the thought. "Please don't make me introduce you to him."

"Hi, good to see you again." Jim greeted, wagging his eyebrows as he leaned against the counter with a hand propped up under his chin.

I wish I had my whip.

"Let's see, what did we mess up this time?" I asked with a sigh, standing behind the desk.

"Well, first of all, I think your staff could treat me better." Jim started as if he had thought up a full list of complaints.

"Well, I'm sorry about that, things have been a bit busy around here lately. As you may know, people aren't beating down the door to be librarians." I tried my best to be nice.

"Other than that, we have to discuss these fines, and I feel all of these are unfair," Jimmy continued, going down his mental list, completely ignoring my response.

I picked the ruler up from the desk in front of me. "Jimmy, we've gone over this. These fines are not profit. We don't put that money in our pocket. They are preset and triggered by the system."

"Okay, I'll give it to you on the fines, but what good is it to have staff if they won't even give me a recommendation? I asked the redhead over there, and she just ignored me."

I glanced around him at Lola, who was making a choking motion. I managed to keep the smirk from my lips. Instead, without thinking, I leaned forward, slapping the ruler against my palm. "Let's straighten a couple of things out here, Jimmy." My voice lowered without pause. "'The redhead has a name, and it's Lola. And I would bet my life on the fact that she didn't just ignore you."

"Well, I…"

I cut him off. "Let me guess, you came rolling in with your mound of books, overdue, waited impatiently, she told you she would be with you in just a moment, and you stomped off in a huff. Am I warm here?"

"Well, the redhead–erm… Lola. She did ask for some time, yes." He stuttered, standing straight from his leisurely leaning position, his eyes nervously staring at the ruler as it slapped my flesh.

" The people here are working awfully hard and don't deserve, nor need, an extra lecture from you. You understand?" I went on. "Furthermore, we will be happy to give you recommendations if you can come in here as a polite and eager library patron, not the overcharged angry guy. Get it?"

"Y-Yeah, I am sorry. I'll try to be better." His tone was nervous and high pitched.

"No, apologizing to me isn't enough. You need to apologize to Lola, and then, only if she accepts, come back here, and I'll give you the recommendations you need." I finished, finally pausing to breathe as he obeyed what I ordered, nodding, and hurrying over to Lola.

"Damn girl, you owned him!" Jennifer whistled as she emerged from the background, patting me on the back. "I'm not sure if I was scared or turned on watching you beat that ruler and put that little man in his place. You just might have a future in the BDSM world."

She laughed as she headed back over to the stacks. A small smirk curved on my lips.

Damn right, I do.